D1242513

Heart of the Forest

Written by: Megan and Lea Deis
Illustrated by: Megan Deis and Viktoriia Maslei

RoseDog Books
PITTSBURGH, PENNSYLVANIA 15238

RoseDog Publishing Co
585 Alpha Drive
Suite 103
Pittsburgh, PA 15238

Visit our website at www.rosedogbookstore.com

ISBN: 978-1-64957-859-4
EISBN: 978-1-64957-879-2

To Sophie, may you grow to be
as adventurous as the Fox, as kind
hearted as the Deer, as generous
as the Bear and as wise as the Owl.
Just know you will never adventure alone.

Fox wants to travel. He has heard that the Heart of the Forest is the most beautiful and peaceful place on earth.

Fox thought this was odd at first. He didn't know that the forest had a heart. Did it also have legs and eyes and a belly too?? But mom had told him about it, and mom was always right, so he knew he had to adventure there.

The very next day, Fox packed his backpack full of snacks, waved goodbye to his mom and dad and began his adventure to the Heart of the Forest.

It wasn't long until he had found a dirt path leading into the woods. He looked up. The sun was shining and there wasn't a cloud in the sky. No matter what happened, Fox knew today was going to be a great day.

After a few minutes, Fox heard a rustling in the leaves. "Hello," he called out, and a beautiful brown creature came out of the trees.

"Hello" the creature called back in a beautiful voice, "I'm Deer! What brings you to the forest?"

Fox thanked his new friend Deer and continued on the trail. It wasn't long until he reached the lake, but Deer didn't tell him about the large creature with long brown fur that was splashing in the water. This creature was so big, it scared Fox and he ran to hide behind a tree.

Fox wanted to turn back, but he had already come this far, so instead he called out "Hello? I'm trying to get to the Heart of the Forest and I have to pass by the lake. Are you friendly?"

"Of course I'm friendly," the creature called out, "My name is Bear! This lake is where I cool off and find my food. Would you like to enjoy a snack with me?"

Fox peered out from the bushes, and saw Bear placing several small fish onto a leaf, ready to eat. Bear then moved over to sit on a large rock and patted the spot next to him for Fox to take a seat.

He looked so friendly, Fox wondered
why he was so scared in the first place.
He took the seat next to Bear and pulled
out a small bag of popcorn and a handful
of licorice out of his backpack.

"So you are headed to the heart?"
Bear asked, "Lucky for you, you are almost
there. Just walk around the lake and through
a patch of very tall trees. When you get
there you'll know."

Fox had listened to Bears words and was almost through the patch of very tall trees. He was getting tired, but he knew he must be close. Suddenly, he heard a "Whooooo. Whooooo." Fox recognized the noise. His dad had told him about the wise old birds that make this sound.

"Owl?? Are you there??"
Fox called out. "I'm looking for the Heart of the Forest?! I've talked to Deer and Bear. They both led me here!"

"Oh, young Fox," Owl replied, "You must be tired. Can't you see, it's just through these bushes!" Fox looked ahead and saw the opening to the heart. He thanked Owl and stepped through the bushes into the most beautiful place he had ever seen.

The bright sun was shining through lush green treetops. Bright yellow and purple wildflowers outlined a small stream that led to a rushing waterfall. His mom was right, the Heart of the Forest was incredible.

Fox was stunned by the beauty that surrounded him, but there was one thought that he couldn't get off his mind. As stunning as the landscape around him was, he wished someone else was there to share in the beauty.

Just as Fox was ready to begin his trek home, he turned around to realize he wasn't alone after all. Deer, Bear and Owl were right behind him, looking around in awe at the heart of the forest in which they lived.

Fox was filled with an overwhelming sense of joy. Although he started this journey alone, he ended it with friends and that's what made it the best adventure of all.

"Hi Deer! I'm looking for the most beautiful part of this forest. Have you heard of it?"

"Oh yes, of course! You must be talking about the heart. Just keep walking on this trail. If you see a lake with lovely blue water, you are on the right path!

Good luck!"

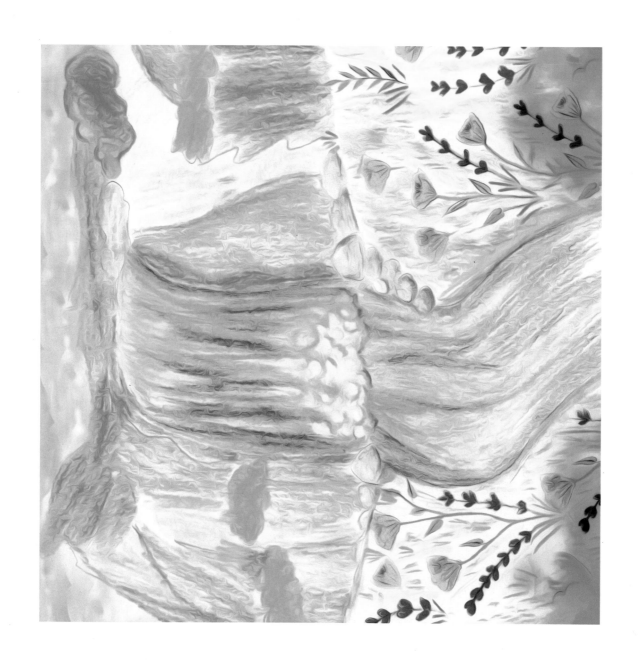